Harlem Ace episode one

Harlem Ace, Volume 1

MR.E

Published by MR.E, 2024.

This is a work of fiction. Similarities to real people, places, or events are entirely coincidental.

HARLEM ACE EPISODE ONE

First edition. November 10, 2024.

Copyright © 2024 MR.E.

ISBN: 979-8227212344

Written by MR.E.

Halem Ace

By MR.E

The morning air hung thick with the cold dampness of Philadelphia in late fall, the kind that seeps through the cracks in the streets and lingers in the breath of the early risers. The city was just beginning to stir, the streetlights flickering off one by one, leaving long, slanted shadows on the sidewalk. Kadin Abell sat at his usual table by the café window, a mug of black coffee steaming between his hands. His broad shoulders hunched slightly, and the brim of his black fedora cast a shadow over his face, concealing a quiet intensity in his dark, watchful eyes.

The café was mostly empty, save for a couple of regulars nursing their own mugs, as the barista moved around lethargically behind the counter. Outside, people passed with hurried steps, bundled in wool coats and scarves, faces downturned against the wind. Kadin barely noticed them. His attention was fixed on the open newspaper in front of him. His fingers traced the edges of the pages as he turned them, slow and deliberate, pausing only when he reached the headline in bold, sinister letters:

"Philly Ripper Strikes Again."

Kadin's jaw tightened as he read. The article below gave a rough outline— "a young woman, early twenties, found in a back alley near the Schuylkill River. Cause of death—multiple stab wounds." His lips pressed together in a hard line. Another victim. The fifth in just three months. He didn't need to read the rest to know what it would say; the details were etched into his mind, as clear as if he'd been there himself. Each victim so far had been young, alone, taken by surprise. The papers loved to speculate, to fill in the blanks with theories and sensationalism, but Kadin knew better than to buy into their hype.

He took a long sip of his coffee, savoring the bitterness that cut through the chill in his bones. Then he sighed, the weight of frustration heavy on his shoulders. Five victims and no closer to understanding why or who. He closed his eyes briefly, as if willing some piece of the puzzle to fall into place, but the image remained stubbornly elusive. His mind, normally so sharp, so adept at weaving disparate facts into cohesive truths, was coming up empty. And each new headline only reminded him of how badly he was failing.

The sharp trill of his cell phone broke through his thoughts. He dug it out of his coat pocket, glancing at the screen before answering. The caller ID read "Chief Waller." Kadin lifted the phone to his ear, his tone neutral, steady.

"Chief."

"Abell," came the gruff voice on the other end, unmistakably Jim Waller, Philadelphia's Chief of Police. Waller's voice carried a familiar roughness, the sound of a man who'd been working nights and drinking his coffee black for far too long.

"I assume you've seen the morning paper?" Waller didn't waste time on pleasantries.

"Yeah, I saw it," Kadin replied, his eyes shifting back to the paper as if the words might suddenly offer up some revelation. "The Philly Ripper strikes again."

Waller exhaled, a sound that was half frustration, half fatigue. "Fifth one, Abell. This one's... bad. Just like the others. Maybe worse."

"Worse?" Kadin's brow furrowed. He had learned long ago not to ask unnecessary questions, but that single word slipped out before he could stop it. Five murders were already far beyond bad. What could be worse?

"She was left out in the open this time," Waller said, his voice low, as if trying to contain something even darker. "Left to be found. And it was... public. People are scared, Kadin. We can't keep holding the press back on this. They're all over us."

Kadin took another sip of his coffee, his eyes narrowing as he considered the chief's words. The Ripper had always been meticulous, careful. Each body had been found hidden, left just out of sight, as if he were trying to delay discovery. This change in method was telling, a deliberate taunt.

"So," Kadin said finally, his voice steady despite the unease coiling in his stomach, "are you calling me in for this one?"

A pause lingered on the other end of the line, just long enough for Kadin to know the answer.

"Yeah. I need you on this, Kadin," Waller said, the tone carrying an unspoken gravity. "All hands on deck, no question about it. Whatever you're working on, drop it. This one's priority."

Kadin nodded, though he knew Waller couldn't see him. "Understood. I'll be there in thirty."

"Good." Waller hesitated, and Kadin could almost see the chief's hand running over his bald head, a nervous tic he'd picked up over the years. "Just... watch yourself. This guy's unpredictable."

The line clicked dead, leaving Kadin with a sense of foreboding that settled heavy in his chest. He slipped the phone back into his pocket, eyes drifting back to the headline one last time. This wasn't just another case, and it wasn't just another killer. The Philly Ripper was different—methodical yet violent, precise yet chaotic. He was playing a game, one that only he knew the rules to, and Kadin hated feeling like he was a step behind, always chasing shadows.

He drained the rest of his coffee, savoring the last bitter dregs, and then folded the newspaper under his arm. As he rose, his trench coat fell in sweeping lines around him, adding to his already formidable presence. Kadin Abell wasn't a man easily rattled, and he'd seen more than his share of darkness in this city. But there was something about the Philly Ripper that felt... wrong, as if he were seeing not just the work of a killer but a reflection of something buried deep within the city itself—its desperation, its despair, its quiet, simmering violence.

He pushed open the café door, stepping out into the morning light. It was muted, filtered through the thick clouds overhead, casting a cold gray hue over everything. Kadin's boots echoed on the sidewalk as he walked, his mind already shifting to what he knew about the previous victims, running over the details like a mantra: young, vulnerable, alone. He'd seen their faces, memorized each photograph as if looking long enough might reveal some hidden clue, something they'd missed the first four times.

The city was waking up around him, indifferent to the dread that hung over it like a storm cloud. Cars crawled along the street, their exhaust rising in thin plumes that vanished into the cold morning air. The regular hum of city life was just beginning, people huddling in coats, hurrying to work, unaware or choosing not to think about the monster that walked among them.

Kadin couldn't afford that luxury.

As he walked, his hand drifted to the inside pocket of his coat, fingers brushing the edge of his badge. He rarely thought of himself as a cop, though he wore the badge and followed orders. He was a hunter, and his prey was men like the Ripper—men who took life without remorse, who killed not out of necessity but out of some twisted need. He knew their type, could almost smell the rot of them in the air.

But the Ripper had a different scent, something elusive, harder to trace. He was careful, too careful, and Kadin knew that unless they found a way into his mind, this game would keep going, the stakes rising with each new victim.

The precinct came into view just ahead, a sturdy, weather-beaten building that had seen as much of Philadelphia's darkness as the men and women inside it. Kadin pulled open the heavy glass door, the warmth of the building hitting him like a wave as he stepped inside. The front desk sergeant glanced up, recognition flashing across his face.

"Abell," he greeted, nodding toward the hallway. "Chief's in his office, been waiting for you."

Kadin gave a brief nod, his face a mask of calm, though his mind was already working through what he might say, what questions he would ask. He made his way down the narrow corridor, his footsteps muffled on the worn carpet. He could feel the eyes of his fellow officers on him, their expressions ranging from curiosity to something close to relief. Everyone knew what he was there for.

He reached the chief's office and knocked once before stepping inside. Chief Waller looked up from his desk, his face lined with exhaustion, eyes heavy with a tension that had been building for months now. He gestured for Kadin to sit.

"Good to see you," Waller said, though the weight in his voice suggested otherwise. "We got a mess on our hands with this one."

Kadin settled into the chair, his gaze steady. "Tell me what you know."

Waller rubbed a hand over his face, sighing deeply. "Not much, unfortunately. Victim's name is Alyssa Torres. Twenty-two years old. Local college student. Found her in an alley behind the diner off Broad Street."

Kadin's eyes narrowed. "Broad Street's a public area. This guy's getting bolder."

"Or reckless," Waller replied, his voice grim. "But we can't count on that. If anything, it seems like he's getting... comfortable. Like he's testing us."

The chief slid a file across the desk, and Kadin picked it up, flipping through the contents. The photographs showed a young woman, her features frozen in fear and pain, her body left in a crumpled heap against a graffiti-scarred wall. His stomach churned, though he kept his expression impassive. He'd seen death before, too many times to count, but the brutality here was something else, something visceral.

"I don't think he's just testing us," Kadin murmured, almost to himself. "I think he's enjoying it."

Waller nodded slowly, his face grim. "Whatever his game is, we're losing. We need to change that, fast."

Kadin's gaze hardened as he closed the file and set it back on the desk. He'd been chasing shadows long enough. This time, he was ready to step into the darkness, to face whatever lay in the depths of this city's soul. The Philly Ripper wouldn't stay in the shadows forever.

"He won't be able to hide much longer," Kadin said quietly, more to himself than to the chief. His voice was steady, almost too calm, but there was an edge beneath it, a sharpness honed by years of hunting monsters in the city's darkest corners.

As he stood and turned toward the door, his hand once again brushing the badge in his coat pocket, Kadin Abell knew one thing with absolute certainty—he would catch the Philly Ripper, no matter what it took.

As Kadin turned to leave Chief Waller's office, his hand barely grazing the doorknob, Jim's voice cut through the silence like a sharpened blade.

"Kadin." The tone was calm, but beneath it, a tension simmered. Kadin froze, casting a glance over his shoulder. Waller's eyes were fixed on him, sharp and unwavering, a caution and a command all rolled into one.

"Keep it in check, you hear me?" Waller's voice dropped, barely above a whisper. "We don't need another... Harker incident."

The words hung heavy in the air, filling the room with a quiet, unspoken weight. Kadin's gaze darkened, but he nodded, his jaw tight. The Harker incident—a name neither man ever spoke unless they absolutely had to. An incident buried so deep it didn't even exist in the precinct records. Only two people knew what had happened that night, what Kadin was capable of when he let his emotions run unchecked. And Jim Waller had been the one to cover it up, to keep the truth from devouring both of them.

"Understood," Kadin said finally, his voice low. He held Waller's gaze for a moment longer, a silent promise exchanged between them. Then, without another word, he slipped out of the office, pulling the door closed behind him with a soft click.

The fluorescent lights buzzed overhead as he strode down the precinct's narrow hallway, his mind drifting back to the Harker incident. He could still see the image as clear as day—the cracked walls, shattered glass scattered like confetti across the floor, the metallic tang of blood in the air. And there, at the center of it all, his own hands clenched in fists, energy thrumming through his veins, electric and raw, like the barely contained charge before a lightning strike.

He blinked, forcing the memory back down, locking it in the place where he kept all his secrets. He didn't have time to relive Harker, not now. The Philly Ripper was out there, and Kadin knew he'd need every ounce of control if he was going to put an end to this.

Outside, the morning had grown colder, a brisk wind slicing through the air as Kadin made his way down the street. His destination was a familiar one—Jimmy's, a small sandwich shop nestled between a laundromat and a pawn shop, both of which had seen better days. Jimmy's had been around longer than most of the buildings on this block, and it had the feel of a place that had earned its right to stay, no matter how rough the neighborhood got.

The neon sign buzzed above the door, casting a faint green glow over the worn sidewalk. Kadin pushed open the door, the bell overhead chiming as he stepped inside. The smell of fresh bread and sizzling bacon hit him immediately, grounding him, if only for a moment.

Behind the counter stood Mark Jimmy, the owner, a burly man with forearms like tree trunks and a mustache that curled at the ends like an old-fashioned handlebar. He looked up as Kadin entered, his face breaking into a grin that was both welcoming and a little rough around the edges.

"Well, look what the cat dragged in," Mark called out, wiping his hands on a stained apron. "Kadin Abell, right on time for the breakfast crowd. Though, I don't think you're here for pancakes."

Kadin managed a half-smile as he approached the counter, pulling a crumpled ten-dollar bill from his pocket and sliding it across to Mark. "Ham and cheese, extra tomato," he said, the words familiar, automatic. He'd been coming to Jimmy's for years now, and Mark knew his order as well as he knew the back of his own hand.

Mark nodded, grabbing a fresh loaf of bread and setting to work, his hands moving with the practiced efficiency of someone who'd been in this business longer than most people had been alive. As he layered the ham and cheese, Kadin leaned against the counter, watching the street outside through the smudged glass window.

"Been a rough week?" Mark asked, his voice gruff but laced with a quiet concern.

Kadin shrugged, his gaze still fixed on the street. "Something like that. You know how it goes."

Mark grunted in agreement, slicing a tomato with quick, precise movements. "You cops have it tougher than most, especially these days." He placed the tomato slices on the sandwich, then looked up, studying Kadin's face with an intensity that caught him off guard.

"You're lookin' a little haunted, Abell," Mark said, his tone softer. "These cases getting to you?"

Kadin's jaw tightened. He didn't like talking about the job, especially not with someone as perceptive as Mark. But the man had earned his respect over the years, and there was a quiet understanding between them, a mutual respect born out of seeing too much and knowing too much.

"It's the same as always," Kadin said after a moment, his voice low. "One step forward, two steps back. Sometimes, you think you're close to something, and then it slips right through your fingers."

Mark nodded, a sympathetic look crossing his face. "It's tough, I get that. But you've got grit, Abell. You're the kind that doesn't back down."

"Sometimes backing down might be the better option," Kadin muttered, mostly to himself. He glanced up, forcing a thin smile. "How's the family?"

A warm smile softened Mark's rough features. "They're good. Boys are growing up faster than weeds, and Sarah keeps telling me I need to take a vacation. But you know me—this place is my vacation."

Kadin chuckled, the sound rough but genuine. He could picture Mark here, even if the world outside fell apart, slinging sandwiches and keeping the doors open. The shop was more than just a business; it was a sanctuary, a place where people could come in off the street and find a little warmth, a little kindness.

"Glad to hear it," Kadin said. He knew Mark had been through his share of hardship, too, that the man's hands weren't just scarred from kitchen work but from years spent fending off the same darkness that haunted the rest of the city.

Mark wrapped the sandwich in a sheet of wax paper, sliding it across the counter. "Here you go. On the house today. You look like you could use a break."

Kadin started to protest, but Mark held up a hand. "Consider it a favor, from one weary soul to another. Besides, you don't come in here nearly enough these days."

With a nod of thanks, Kadin accepted the sandwich, tucking it under his arm. He could feel the comforting warmth through his coat, a small reminder that there were still simple things in life, things untouched by the violence and chaos lurking outside.

As he turned to leave, Mark called out after him, his voice softer than before. "You take care of yourself, Abell. We don't need any more Harker incidents."

Kadin paused, his back to the counter, feeling a chill snake up his spine. The words carried a weight that was almost tangible, a reminder that even those who weren't supposed to know seemed to sense the darkness he held within. He didn't turn around, didn't acknowledge the statement. He simply gave a slight nod, then stepped outside, back into the cold embrace of the city.

The street was quiet, but Kadin could feel the undercurrent of tension, the unspoken fear that had settled over Philadelphia like a heavy fog. People walked briskly, heads down, trying to avoid eye contact, as if acknowledging each other might somehow make them a target. The Philly Ripper had cast a long shadow, one that stretched across every corner of the city, infecting it with a fear that felt almost alive.

Kadin's mind drifted back to Harker, that night buried deep in the past. It had been a disaster, a raw, chaotic moment when he'd let the full force of his powers loose, unable to contain the fury bubbling inside. Walls had buckled, objects had torn themselves apart, and the air had crackled with an electric hum that left his skin tingling long after. In the end, he had walked out alive, but what he'd left behind was... unrecognizable.

The Harker incident had taught him a harsh lesson—that his abilities weren't just a gift but a double-edged sword, a weapon that, if unchecked, could do more harm than good. It was why he kept himself in control, why he forced his emotions into tight boxes, never allowing them to overflow. The city couldn't afford a cop who was as dangerous as the criminals he hunted.

The sandwich shop door closed behind him with a gentle jingle, the warmth of Jimmy's quickly replaced by the biting chill of the morning. Kadin walked down the sidewalk, the weight of Waller's words pressing down on him with each step. His telekinetic abilities were a secret he'd guarded closely, a secret known to only a handful of people, and Waller was one of them. The chief's warning hadn't just been about keeping the Ripper at bay; it was about keeping the other, darker part of himself in check.

As he walked, he unwrapped the sandwich, taking a bite as he let the familiar flavors ground him. The bread was fresh, the ham salty, the tomato adding a hint of sweetness. For a moment, he allowed himself to sink into the simplicity of it, a small respite from the chaos that waited for him.

But he couldn't shake the feeling that the Ripper case was pushing him closer to the edge, closer to that dark place he'd tried so hard to avoid since Harker. He knew, deep down, that he was hunting a predator, one as cunning and ruthless as any he'd faced before. And the city, always unforgiving, would demand answers, justice, blood.

He finished the sandwich, brushing the crumbs off his coat as he turned the corner, the precinct looming in the distance. The city watched him, its gaze unyielding, its shadows deep and unforgiving. He had a job to do, a killer to catch, and he knew it would take everything he had—maybe even more than he was willing to give.

With one last look over his shoulder, Kadin stepped forward, the weight of his past and the darkness of his power trailing behind him like a second shadow. And as he walked, the city seemed to hold its breath, waiting for the next move in a game that felt as old as time itself.

CHAPTER 2

Kadin's boots hit the pavement with a slow, measured rhythm as he made his way down the city's grimy sidewalk. The morning's coffee buzz had faded, replaced by a creeping unease that nestled into his bones. He was just a few blocks away from the precinct, but something felt... off. It was the kind of feeling he'd learned to trust, an instinct honed over years of walking these streets.

He tugged his trench coat closer against the chill, keeping his face neutral, his eyes scanning the reflections in the shop windows as he passed. No one unusual. Just the typical scattering of people—the woman with the shopping bags, the guy reading his phone, the older man hobbling with a cane. But the feeling only grew stronger, a persistent itch at the base of his skull.

Kadin exhaled slowly, deciding to test his suspicions. He veered left down a narrow alleyway, a route he wouldn't normally take but one he knew would give him a chance to confirm if someone was indeed tailing him. The alley was shadowed and damp, the kind of place where the stench of garbage mixed with the faint, metallic tang of rust. He kept his pace slow, deliberate, not wanting to tip off whoever might be watching.

As he moved deeper into the alley, the sense of being followed intensified. He kept his breathing steady, eyes forward, listening for any telltale signs of footsteps or shuffling behind him. But there was nothing—just an eerie silence that hung in the air, broken only by the occasional drip of water from a pipe overhead.

Then, without warning, a cold, invisible grip closed around his shoulder. Kadin's muscles seized up, and he froze, the air in his lungs turning cold. He tried to turn, to face whoever—or whatever—had touched him, but his body refused to move. It was as if he'd been locked in place, every muscle stiffened, frozen by an unseen force.

His heart pounded as he strained against the paralysis, his mind racing. Then he felt it—a whisper, close to his ear, a voice low and smooth, with an edge of menace that sent a chill down his spine.

"Stay out of my business, Kadin," the voice murmured, the sound soft but laced with a venom that left no room for misinterpretation. "You don't have to suffer like the others."

The voice was unmistakably female, and each word dripped with a kind of confidence, a chilling certainty. It was calm, unhurried, the voice of someone who knew exactly what she was doing.

And then, just as quickly as the paralysis had come, it vanished. Kadin stumbled forward, catching himself against the alley wall, his breathing harsh and erratic as he struggled to regain control. He whirled around, expecting to see someone standing there, but the alley was empty. Only shadows greeted him, stretching out in silent mockery.

He pressed a hand against his shoulder, as if expecting to feel some lingering trace of the grip that had held him in place, but there was nothing. Just his own pulse, still hammering beneath his skin.

The Philly Ripper. It had to be her. No one else would have the audacity, the control, to pull something like that. But the realization brought with it an even more disturbing thought. If she had done this—if she'd paralyzed him, made her presence known and then vanished without a trace—then she wasn't just a cold-blooded killer. She was like him, a meta, someone with abilities beyond the norm.

His mind spun with the implications, questions piling on top of each other with dizzying speed. How long had she been watching him? Was she trying to intimidate him, scare him off the case? Or was there something deeper at play, some twisted game she was pulling him into?

Kadin took a shaky breath, glancing around the alley once more before heading back toward the main street. He needed answers, but he knew he wouldn't find them here. Whatever game the Ripper was playing, she held the cards. But if she thought a whispered warning and a show of power would be enough to scare him off, she was wrong. This wasn't his first time facing someone like her.

He squared his shoulders, forcing his breathing to steady as he retraced his steps toward the precinct. Each step was deliberate, purposeful, a silent promise to himself. The Ripper had crossed a line, made it personal, and he wasn't going to let her slip through his fingers.

By the time he reached the precinct, the weight of what had just happened still pressed heavily on him, but his expression remained calm, a mask honed from years of keeping his emotions in check. He pushed open the precinct doors and strode down the familiar hallway, making his way to Jim Waller's office. He tapped lightly on the door before stepping inside, shutting it quietly behind him.

Waller looked up from his desk, his brow furrowing as he took in Kadin's expression. "You look like you've seen a ghost."

Kadin gave a short, humorless laugh. "Not a ghost," he said, dropping into the chair across from Waller. "But close enough."

Waller's eyes narrowed. He knew Kadin well enough to recognize when something serious was going on. "What happened?"

Kadin leaned forward, keeping his voice low. "I was walking down Market, and I got this feeling… like I was being followed. Took a detour into an alley, just to be sure. And that's when it happened."

He paused, trying to find the right words to describe the sensation. "I felt this… grip on my shoulder. I couldn't move, couldn't even turn around. And then there was this voice. A woman's voice, whispering in my ear, telling me to stay out of her business."

Waller's expression grew darker with each word. He folded his hands in front of him, listening intently, his eyes sharp and calculating.

Kadin continued, his voice tense. "She let me go after a few seconds, and when I turned, there was no one there. I don't know how, but I'm sure it was her—the Philly Ripper."

Waller leaned back in his chair, rubbing a hand over his face. "You're telling me she's a meta too?"

"It would explain how she's been able to stay ahead of us," Kadin replied, his jaw tight. "If she has some kind of telepathic or telekinetic abilities, she could be using them to avoid capture, to manipulate evidence, hell, even to stay out of sight entirely."

Waller was silent, absorbing the information, his eyes never leaving Kadin's. Finally, he spoke, his voice low and laced with frustration. "You know this complicates things. If she's a meta... then we're dealing with something way beyond a normal killer. We don't even know the extent of her abilities."

Kadin nodded, the weight of the situation settling heavily on him. "She's bold, Jim. She wanted me to know she's watching. Wanted to make sure I knew that she can find me anytime she wants."

Waller let out a long breath, shaking his head. "And you're sure she's the Ripper?"

"I'm sure," Kadin replied, his voice firm. "This wasn't just a random warning. She mentioned others suffering. Who else could she be talking about?"

Waller's jaw clenched, his gaze hard. "So what now?"

Kadin met his eyes, his own gaze steady. "We can't treat this like an ordinary case. We're dealing with someone who's not just dangerous but has an edge we can't predict. We need to be prepared for anything."

Waller's face softened for a moment, his worry breaking through. "Kadin... you know what this means. If she's a meta and she's this powerful, she might be able to—"

"I know," Kadin cut him off, not wanting to give voice to the darker thoughts lingering in both their minds. He'd spent years keeping his own powers in check, hiding them from most people, knowing how dangerous they could be if unleashed. If the Ripper was half as strong as she seemed, then she was a threat unlike any he'd faced before.

Waller drummed his fingers on the desk, the tension thick in the room. "All right," he said finally, his voice laced with determination. "We're not backing down. But I need you to stay sharp, Kadin. If she's watching, if she's targeting you, then you need to keep a low profile. Don't give her an inch."

Kadin nodded, his face set. "I know the stakes, Jim. And I'm not going to let her get away with this."

They sat in silence for a moment, the weight of their shared resolve filling the room. The Ripper might have the upper hand for now, but Kadin knew he couldn't afford to let fear or uncertainty cloud his judgment. She'd made a mistake by approaching him, by revealing her presence.

And now, more than ever, Kadin was determined to turn the tables.

"Let's get to work," he said finally, his voice steady and resolute. Waller nodded, a faint glimmer of approval in his eyes.

Kadin left the office, his mind already working, sifting through what little they knew, trying to find some thread he could pull. He'd faced darkness before, but this was something else, something deeper, a malevolence that seemed to lurk just outside his reach.

But he wouldn't stop. Not until he'd put an end to it.

Later that night…

The warehouse was a forgotten relic on the outskirts of Philadelphia, hidden behind crumbling walls and long-abandoned train tracks. It was a place the city had left to rot, and now it stood like a monument to decay, its metal walls rusted, windows shattered, and silence so thick it felt suffocating.

Inside, a single bulb hung from the rafters, casting a dull yellow glow across the makeshift space below. Dust floated in the air, disturbed only by the faint sound of footsteps echoing against the cold concrete floor.

The Philly Ripper appeared out of nowhere, materializing like a wraith from the shadows. She was tall and lean, her figure concealed beneath a fitted red police uniform jacket, its fabric clean and crisp against the grimy backdrop of the warehouse. A green cap sat atop her head, and worn sneakers of the same shade covered her feet. The contrast of her bright clothing in this place of neglect was striking, as if she'd come dressed not for stealth, but for defiance.

Her steps were deliberate as she crossed the floor to a low, sagging couch positioned against one of the walls. She lay down slowly, stretching her legs out, her head sinking back into the tattered cushions as she exhaled a long, steady sigh. Her heart was pounding, a strange and exhilarating beat that she couldn't seem to calm, a remnant from her encounter with Kadin Abell that morning. The thrill of it pulsed through her veins, the memory of his presence so close, his warmth just a hair's breadth away, tantalizingly out of reach.

Her hand drifted to the pocket of her red jacket, pulling out a sleek black phone. She held it above her, the cracked screen catching the dim light, and unlocked it with a quick flick of her thumb. She navigated to her photo gallery, her fingers moving with practiced ease, until a mosaic of images filled the screen.

Each one was a snapshot of Kadin, taken from a distance, his silhouette sharp and unmistakable. She had captured him in every conceivable setting—walking through crowded streets, leaning against his car, sitting at a café, his fedora tipped low over his eyes as he read the morning paper. A few images were closer, more intimate; his hand wrapped around a coffee cup, his eyes narrowed as he studied something off-camera, his profile cast in the soft glow of twilight.

Her heart raced as she scrolled through them, her pulse quickening with each swipe. She knew every detail of his face, every nuance in his expressions, every shade of emotion that flickered behind his dark eyes. She had watched him for weeks now, learning his patterns, studying his movements, memorizing his habits. But for her, this was more than mere observation. She felt a pull toward him, a connection that defied explanation. She couldn't place why, but she felt as if they were bound together by something neither of them could fully understand.

A faint smile curled at the edges of her lips as she paused on a photo of him taken just a few days earlier. He had been standing outside the precinct, his face turned up toward the early morning sky, his expression contemplative. The moment had struck her—his face softened in a rare, unguarded moment, a glimpse of vulnerability that he rarely showed to the world. She traced her finger along the outline of his face, as if she could reach through the screen and touch him.

But her smile faded as she remembered the encounter earlier that morning, the way he had reacted to her touch, the fear and surprise that had flickered in his eyes. She'd been careful to keep her distance until now, never approaching him directly, content to observe from the shadows. But something had compelled her to break that silence, to feel his presence up close, to test the boundaries of the connection she felt.

She didn't know why he fascinated her, why his every move seemed to pull her in like a magnet. It wasn't love, no, she knew that much. Love was a shallow thing, fleeting and insubstantial. What she felt was something deeper, more primal, a curiosity that gnawed at her, demanding answers that even she couldn't fully articulate.

Kadin Abell. The name itself felt heavy, filled with meaning, a name she'd whispered to herself in the quiet hours of the night as she lay alone in this decaying sanctuary. He was like her, she sensed that, though he kept his abilities hidden beneath a layer of control that she found both admirable and infuriating. She could feel the power radiating off him, a restrained energy that simmered just below the surface, begging to be unleashed. She wanted to see it, wanted to know what he was capable of when he let himself go, when he embraced the darkness that lurked inside him.

Her fingers tightened around the phone, her nails pressing into the cold metal casing as her mind replayed the encounter. She had left him a warning, a gentle nudge to steer clear, to let her be. But she knew he wouldn't listen. He was too stubborn, too determined. He would keep coming, keep digging, no matter how many barriers she put in his way.

And maybe... maybe that was exactly what she wanted.

She lay back on the couch, her fingers tapping idly on the phone screen as she scrolled through the gallery once more. The images were like pieces of a puzzle, fragments of a story that only she could see. Kadin was a mystery, a beautiful, complex enigma that she yearned to unravel. She wanted to peel back the layers, to see what lay beneath that stoic exterior, to understand the thoughts that flickered behind his guarded eyes.

She laughed softly, a sound that echoed through the empty warehouse, hollow and sharp. "Kadin," she whispered, letting the name roll off her tongue like a prayer, or perhaps a curse. "You don't know what you're getting yourself into."

The thrill of the hunt stirred within her, a familiar sensation that sent a shiver of anticipation down her spine. She was the Philly Ripper, a specter that haunted the city's darkest corners, a ghost who left no trace. She had evaded them all, danced circles around their investigations, leading them on a chase they would never win. But Kadin was different. He was no ordinary cop. He was something else, something that made her blood sing with excitement and fear in equal measure.

She had sensed his powers, felt the way they hummed beneath the surface, restrained but potent. He was like her, a meta, someone who understood the thrill of holding that kind of power, of wielding it with precision and purpose. She could feel it, a strange resonance that connected them, like two pieces of the same broken mirror.

As she lay there, staring at his image, she wondered if he knew just how much they were alike. He hid his powers, kept them bottled up, leashed by the rules and restraints of his profession. But she knew that under the right pressure, he would break, that he would unleash that power with the same ferocity she felt coursing through her own veins. And when that happened... well, she wanted to be there to see it.

A sense of satisfaction filled her as she closed the gallery, her fingers lingering over the screen. She'd let him see her, let him feel her presence. It was a calculated risk, one that could have backfired, but she knew that every move had to be precise, every step carefully planned. She didn't want him to run. No, she wanted him to come after her, to follow her deeper into the labyrinth she had created. This was her game, and she had set the rules.

She slipped the phone back into her pocket, her heart still beating faster than usual. There was a thrill in the chase, a delicious tension that hung in the air, thick and heady. Kadin was getting closer, and she knew that soon, their paths would cross in a way that neither of them could predict.

But for now, she would wait, hidden in the shadows, watching, always watching. She would continue her work, leaving her trail of bodies across the city, taunting him, daring him to find her. And when the time was right, when she was ready, she would reveal herself fully, let him see the truth of who she was and why she had chosen him.

She lay back on the couch, her eyes drifting to the broken ceiling above, where the faint light of the morning sun filtered through cracks in the roof. She felt at peace here, in this forgotten place, a sanctuary where she could slip in and out of the world without a trace.

With a final sigh, she closed her eyes, letting the memory of Kadin's face fill her mind. She was patient, after all. She could wait as long as it took.

Because one thing was certain—Kadin Abell was hers, whether he realized it or not. And when the time came, he would understand the truth, understand the connection that bound them.

And until then, she would be waiting, lurking in the shadows, her gaze fixed on him, a predator watching her prey, knowing that sooner or later, he would come to her.

And when he did... well, that was when the real game would

CHAPTER 3

M eanwhile...
The night was calm, and the city's hum had settled into a muted, distant buzz, like the last breaths of a long, exhausting day. Kadin Abell sat alone at his small dining table, a dim lamp casting a warm glow over the wooden surface. In front of him, the morning's newspaper lay open, its corners curled slightly, the ink smudged from his fingers. He sipped his cup of decaf coffee—his nighttime ritual, a last bit of warmth before the solitude of the evening closed in completely.

The article he was reading recounted the recent spike in crime, but his mind kept drifting back to the Philly Ripper. She'd been silent since their last encounter, a haunting presence that lingered on the edge of his consciousness, her warning echoing in his mind. Kadin had spent the past few days combing through evidence, working late nights at the precinct, but the Ripper had slipped back into the shadows, leaving no trace. Her words, however, still clung to him like a cold mist. He took another sip of coffee, trying to push her from his mind.

The shrill ring of his phone shattered the quiet, its suddenness jolting him out of his thoughts. Kadin frowned, glancing at the screen. It was a number he didn't recognize, and his first thought was that it was probably a scam call. Half of him wanted to ignore it, but a nagging feeling made him hesitate. The Ripper had a way of infiltrating his life, worming into his thoughts, and now, for some reason he couldn't explain, this call felt different.

With a sigh, he pressed the answer button, holding the phone to his ear.

"Hello?"

For a brief moment, there was only silence on the other end, the kind that felt intentionally placed, heavy and expectant. And then, a soft voice floated through the line, smooth and laced with a chilling familiarity.

"Hello, Kadin."

His blood ran cold. He recognized the voice instantly, that low, mocking tone that had whispered in his ear in the alley. The Philly Ripper.

He fought to keep his voice steady, hiding the surprise that threatened to crack through his calm exterior. "How did you get this number?" he asked, though he knew it was a pointless question. She was toying with him, and whatever rules he thought applied didn't matter to her.

A soft laugh, light and airy, drifted through the line. "Come on, Kadin. You know better than that."

Kadin's grip tightened around the phone, a spark of anger flaring in his chest. She had managed to get closer than anyone ever had, slipping past every boundary he'd set up, invading his life as easily as slipping on a new disguise. He'd spent days trying to track her, unravel her identity, but here she was, calling him, as if she were the one leading the investigation.

"What do you want?" he asked, his voice low, edged with frustration. He wasn't in the mood to play games.

"Oh, don't sound so angry, Kadin," she purred. "I just wanted to check in. After all, you seemed so tense the last time we met. I thought maybe we could... clear the air."

He resisted the urge to lash out, keeping his tone measured. "We didn't meet. You ambushed me."

She laughed again, a sound as cold as the city's winter air. "Ambush, meet—such harsh words. I was simply making my presence known. You're quite the captivating subject, after all."

Her words twisted something deep inside him, an uneasy mix of anger and curiosity. This wasn't just a killer taunting a cop. There was something personal here, something that went beyond the typical cat-and-mouse game. She was watching him, studying him, and he had no idea why.

"What's your game?" he demanded, unable to keep the edge out of his voice. "Why me?"

There was a pause, and for a moment he thought she might actually answer, that she might let him glimpse the truth hidden behind the mask. But when she spoke again, her tone was playful, teasing, as if she enjoyed watching him grasp at answers he couldn't reach.

"Now, now, Kadin," she said, her voice softening into a near whisper. "It wouldn't be any fun if I just told you, would it? You're a detective. You should know by now that the chase is the best part."

He clenched his jaw, his patience wearing thin. "People are dead. This isn't a game."

"Oh, but it is, Kadin. And you're playing it with me, whether you want to or not."

The words hung between them, a challenge, a twisted invitation that made his skin crawl. He'd dealt with killers before, but she was different. She wasn't driven by desperation or anger; she seemed to thrive on the thrill, to savor every moment of her gruesome work. And somehow, she'd drawn him into her world, forcing him to play by rules he didn't understand.

"You're sick," he spat, unable to keep the disgust out of his voice. "And I'm going to catch you. You won't get away with this."

For the first time, her tone shifted, a hint of something darker slipping into her voice. "Oh, Kadin... Do you really think you're in control here?"

He opened his mouth to respond, but the words died on his lips as she continued, her voice softer, almost tender. "You have no idea what I'm capable of. Or what you're capable of, for that matter."

He stiffened, a chill running down his spine. "What are you talking about?"

"Come now, Kadin. I know you feel it—the power inside you. That burning need to break free from all those chains you've wrapped around yourself." Her words were like poison, seeping into his mind, stirring thoughts he'd buried long ago.

"You don't know anything about me," he said, though his voice lacked the conviction he wanted it to have. She had touched something raw, something he'd tried to keep hidden, even from himself.

"Oh, but I do," she replied, her tone soft, almost intimate. "I know you better than you think. And I know that if you let yourself, you'd be just like me."

A knot formed in his stomach, a sick feeling twisting through him as her words sank in. She was trying to manipulate him, to pull him into her web, and he knew it. But there was something about her voice, the way she spoke with such certainty, that made him doubt himself. She was getting under his skin, peeling away layers he'd thought were impenetrable.

"You're wrong," he said, though the words felt hollow. "I'm nothing like you."

"Oh, Kadin," she murmured, a hint of disappointment in her voice. "You keep telling yourself that. But I see the truth. I see the darkness in you, the same darkness that drives me. You can try to run from it, but eventually, you'll have to face it."

He felt the urge to hang up, to sever the connection and end this twisted conversation, but he couldn't bring himself to do it. She'd ensnared him, her words pulling him in deeper, like a moth drawn to a flame.

"Why are you doing this?" he asked finally, his voice barely above a whisper. "What do you want from me?"

Her answer was simple, and yet it sent a shiver through him. "I want you to understand."

The line went silent for a moment, and he thought she might have hung up. But then her voice returned, softer, almost wistful.

"You have so much potential, Kadin. But you waste it, hiding behind rules and limitations, pretending to be something you're not. I'm just here to show you the truth."

"Truth?" he repeated, the word bitter on his tongue. "You think killing innocent people is some kind of truth?"

"Life is a game, Kadin. We're all just players, some of us with more freedom than others. I've accepted that. And you... you could too."

He swallowed, struggling to keep his voice steady. "I don't want your freedom."

"Are you sure?" Her voice was a gentle taunt, dripping with a dark amusement. "Because I think you do. I think you want to break free, to let go of all that control you cling to. I think, deep down, you want to see what you're truly capable of."

He felt his heart pounding, each beat echoing in his chest like a warning. She was playing with him, twisting his own thoughts against him, planting seeds of doubt that he knew would be hard to shake. But he couldn't let her win. He couldn't let her drag him down to her level.

"You don't know me," he said, his voice stronger this time. "You're just a coward hiding behind a mask, killing people because it's the only way you feel powerful. But that's not strength. That's weakness."

There was a long pause, and for a moment he thought he'd struck a nerve. But when she spoke again, her voice was colder, harder, stripped of its previous warmth.

"You're wrong, Kadin. I don't kill because I need to. I kill because I want to. There's a difference."

Her words sent a shiver through him, the stark honesty of them chilling him to the core. This wasn't just a game to her. This was her truth, a twisted reality she embraced without shame or remorse.

"Goodbye, Kadin," she said, her tone almost mocking. "I'll be seeing you soon."

And with that, the line went dead, leaving him alone in the silence.

He stared at the phone in his hand, his mind racing, his heart pounding in his chest. The Philly Ripper had found a way into his life, into his thoughts, and he knew that this was only the beginning. She had drawn a line in the sand, dared him to cross it, and he could feel the weight of her words pressing down on him, pulling him toward a darkness he'd spent his whole life avoiding.

But he wouldn't let her win. He wouldn't let her corrupt him, no matter how seductive her words, no matter how tempting the freedom she offered.

Setting the phone down, he took a deep breath, grounding himself in the quiet of his apartment. The battle had begun, and he knew that it would be a war fought not just in the streets, but in his own mind.

And the Philly Ripper would soon learn that Kadin Abell wasn't as easy to break as she might think.

The following morning, Kadin Abell entered the Philadelphia Police Department with a grim determination etched into his face. His mind was still churning from the call he'd received the night before, the haunting voice of the Philly Ripper lingering like a shadow he couldn't shake. The implications were troubling—if she could get his number, how close had she really gotten? It was a question he didn't want to answer alone.

Without wasting time, Kadin made his way down the bustling hallway, his boots echoing on the tile floor as he approached Chief Waller's office. He knocked once before stepping inside, closing the door quietly behind him. The chief looked up from his paperwork, a mix of surprise and curiosity crossing his face.

"Abell," Waller greeted, setting his pen down and crossing his arms over his chest. "Something on your mind?"

Kadin took a breath, bracing himself. "I need access to the station's surveillance footage from last night."

Waller's brows knitted together in confusion. "Surveillance footage? Why?"

Kadin hesitated, choosing his words carefully. "I got a call late last night. From a number I didn't recognize at first. I thought it was just a scam, but when I picked up..." He paused, his eyes darkening as he remembered the female voice that had spoken his name with such chilling familiarity. "It was her, Chief. The Ripper. She called me."

Waller's eyes widened, and he leaned forward, his gaze sharpening. "You're telling me the Philly Ripper has your personal number?"

Kadin nodded, keeping his expression steady. "It's worse than that. I recognized the number after the call. It came from one of the phones registered to the evidence locker. I think someone broke into the station last night."

Waller's expression turned stormy, a mix of anger and concern flashing across his face. "Are you certain about this, Abell? The Ripper getting into our station? Do you know what you're saying?"

"Dead certain," Kadin replied. "I double-checked the caller ID this morning. I know the evidence locker phones, and that's where the call came from. If she was here... she was close, Chief. Closer than we thought."

The chief sat back in his chair, processing the information. His gaze drifted to the door, as if he were mentally scanning the station's layout, imagining all the places someone could slip through undetected. After a moment, he refocused on Kadin, his jaw tight.

"All right," he said, his voice carrying a newfound edge. "You'll get access to the cameras. But Abell..." He leaned forward, his gaze piercing. "If she was here, if she somehow got into the evidence locker... then we've got a problem bigger than either of us realized."

Kadin nodded. "That's why I need to know for sure. She could be taunting us, slipping in just to leave breadcrumbs. But if she's accessing our equipment, there's no telling what she could have done while she was here."

Waller didn't hesitate further. He stood, grabbing his keys from his desk and gesturing for Kadin to follow him. They made their way through the narrow hallways toward the security room, the atmosphere tense. Officers passed by, nodding greetings or giving curious glances, but neither Kadin nor Waller broke their pace. They both knew that the Ripper had crossed a line. If she was infiltrating the station itself, she wasn't just a threat outside; she was a danger within their very walls.

When they reached the security room, Waller punched in the access code and stepped inside. The room was small and dimly lit, the walls lined with monitors displaying various angles of the station. A young officer sat at the console, monitoring the live feeds, but he looked up as they entered, surprise crossing his face.

"Chief, Abell," he greeted, nodding. "What brings you down here?"

"We need the footage from last night," Waller said briskly. "Start at 10 PM and run it until 2 AM. Focus on the evidence room corridor."

The officer's eyebrows lifted slightly, but he nodded, tapping a few keys to bring up the requested footage. The screen split, showing different camera angles from the evidence room's hallway and adjacent areas. Kadin watched intently, his gaze fixed on the screen as they began scrubbing through the footage.

The first hour passed in silence. The hallway was mostly empty, save for the occasional officer passing by, heading home or finishing up paperwork. The faint glow of the monitor cast harsh shadows over Kadin's face as he leaned forward, studying every movement, every flicker of shadow on the screen. Waller stood beside him, equally focused, his arms crossed tightly over his chest.

Then, just after midnight, something caught Kadin's eye. A figure appeared in the hallway, moving with a careful, almost calculated grace. The figure was cloaked in shadows, their face obscured by the angle of the camera, but there was something about the way they moved—silent, fluid, as if they knew exactly where the cameras were.

"There," Kadin murmured, pointing to the screen. "Pause it."

The officer froze the footage, and they all leaned closer. The figure stood at the end of the hallway, just outside the evidence room door, their form barely illuminated by the overhead lights. Though their face was hidden, the figure's posture, the way they held themselves, felt familiar. The Ripper. He could feel it.

"Play it," Waller instructed, his voice low.

The figure moved with a smooth efficiency, reaching into a pocket and pulling out something small and dark—a keycard, by the looks of it. They swiped it across the scanner, the door clicking open. The Ripper slipped inside without hesitation, the door swinging shut behind them.

Kadin clenched his fists, his mind racing. "She has a keycard. But how?"

Waller's jaw tightened. "No one unauthorized has access to those. Either she stole it... or she's getting help from the inside."

The thought settled heavily between them, the implications both chilling and infuriating. Kadin's mind reeled at the possibilities. If the Ripper had an accomplice, someone inside the station, it would explain how she'd managed to stay one step ahead of them. But the thought of a mole, someone betraying their own, made his blood boil.

"Keep playing," Waller said, his voice hard.

The footage resumed, showing the empty hallway. Minutes passed, then the door to the evidence room clicked open again, and the figure emerged, slipping back into the hallway. But this time, something was different. In their hand, they held a small object—too small to make out clearly on the grainy screen, but unmistakably one of the evidence locker phones.

The Ripper paused, her face turning slightly toward the camera, as if sensing she was being watched. Her features were still obscured, a shadow hiding every detail, but her posture exuded a chilling confidence. She raised the phone to her ear, her head tilting slightly, as if listening.

Kadin felt a shiver run down his spine. That was the moment she'd called him. She had been right there, in their station, calling him from a phone that should have been secure, her voice slipping through the line like a poison.

The footage continued, showing the Ripper lowering the phone and slipping it back into the locker before closing the door. She turned and walked back down the hallway, disappearing into the shadows, as if she'd never been there at all.

Silence filled the room as the footage ended, each of them processing what they had just seen. Waller's face was dark, his jaw clenched, his fists balled at his sides. Kadin's mind raced, replaying the events, the sense of violation washing over him in waves. She'd been inside their sanctuary, had breached the very place where he was supposed to be safe, and she'd done it with an ease that sent a chill through him.

"She's mocking us," Waller said finally, his voice rough. "She wanted you to know she was here, Abell. This was no accident."

Kadin nodded slowly, his eyes narrowing. "She knows we're watching, and she doesn't care. She wants me to chase her. It's a game to her, and she's making the rules."

The chief turned to the officer at the console. "Make a copy of this footage and store it on an encrypted drive. No one sees this except us. Got it?"

The officer nodded, his face pale, and set to work. Waller turned back to Kadin, his expression hard and determined.

"We can't ignore this, Abell. If she has access to our resources, she's more dangerous than we realized. I want every officer briefed. No one goes anywhere without their badge and keycard, and if anyone loses track of their equipment, I want to know immediately."

Kadin nodded, though his mind was already turning over his next move. The Ripper had left a message, one far more potent than just a voice on the other end of a call. She had breached his world, his sanctuary, and he couldn't shake the feeling that she was leading him somewhere, drawing him closer with every taunt, every threat.

"I'll double down on my investigation," he said, his voice steady. "She wants my attention? She's got it."

Waller nodded approvingly, though there was a hint of worry in his eyes. "Be careful, Abell. She's got her claws in deep, and I don't want you getting dragged down with her."

Kadin met the chief's gaze, a silent determination in his own. "I'm not going to let her win, Chief. She's taunted us for long enough."

They left the security room together, each of them lost in their own thoughts. As Kadin walked back toward his office, he could feel the weight of the Ripper's challenge pressing down on him, a dark presence lurking just outside his reach. She was daring him to find her, to uncover the truth she'd hidden beneath layers of shadows and lies.

But this time, he wouldn't hold back. He'd dig deeper, push harder, and if he had to, he'd use every ounce of his own power to track her down.

Because the Ripper had made a fatal error—she'd underestimated him. And Kadin Abell was no stranger to the darkness.

CHAPTER 4

Four hours later...

Kadin Abell walked through the city streets, his steps falling into the quiet rhythm of Philadelphia's early morning. The sky was painted a steely gray, the kind that blurred the line between night and dawn. It was as if the city itself had held its breath, suspended in the last moments of calm before the rush of the day began.

But Kadin's mind was far from calm. The events of the past few days weighed on him heavily, and the call from the Ripper still echoed in his thoughts, each word crawling through his mind like an insidious vine. He couldn't shake the feeling that he was walking into her trap, that she had lured him into a game where she held all the cards.

As he rounded a corner, his footfall paused, and a strange, familiar feeling washed over him—an echo from the past. His pulse quickened, and he found himself back in a different time, a different place, memories he'd tried to bury clawing their way to the surface.

The Harker incident. It had been years ago, but the memory was vivid, burned into his mind with a clarity that hadn't faded.

He could still feel the cold night air on his skin, still hear the low hum of electricity that had crackled through his veins that night.

In his mind, he was there again.

The night was dark, the moon hidden behind thick clouds that blotted out the stars, casting the world into shadow. Kadin had been called to a run-down building on the outskirts of the city, a place where even the streetlights refused to shine, leaving the streets bathed in an eerie, unnatural darkness. The place reeked of neglect, the walls damp with mildew and graffiti, the windows shattered and empty, like hollow eyes watching his every move.

Harker had been waiting for him inside, a man Kadin had been tracking for weeks. Known to the force as a violent and sadistic criminal, Harker had managed to evade arrest time and time again. But Kadin had finally caught up with him, cornered him in the darkened building where he'd made his last stand.

Kadin remembered the way his heart had raced as he'd stepped into the building, his flashlight barely illuminating the darkness. He'd moved through the maze of rooms, his every sense alert, the adrenaline surging through him like a second heartbeat.

And then, he'd found him.

Harker had been standing in the center of a large, empty room, his back to Kadin, his body silhouetted against the faint glow coming from a window high above. The room had an unnatural silence to it, the kind that made every small sound seem amplified, each breath a deafening roar.

Harker hadn't flinched as Kadin had approached, his calm demeanor unnerving, as if he'd been expecting him all along.

There was something about the man's presence that felt wrong, an unsettling aura that made Kadin's skin crawl.

When Harker finally turned to face him, Kadin had felt a flicker of something he rarely experienced—fear. The man's eyes were dark, cold, and filled with a twisted kind of satisfaction, as if he knew a secret Kadin couldn't possibly understand.

"You're late, Detective," Harker had said, his voice low and mocking, carrying a dark edge that sent a shiver down Kadin's spine.

Kadin had raised his weapon, his voice steady but his mind racing. "It's over, Harker. There's nowhere left to run."

Harker's smile had widened, and he'd taken a step forward, his gaze locked on Kadin with an intensity that felt like a physical weight pressing down on him. "Run? Oh, Detective, I've been waiting for you. You think this is a simple arrest, a routine capture?"

Kadin had tightened his grip on his gun, every instinct telling him to stay alert, to be ready for anything. But Harker's presence had been overpowering, like a dark force that filled the room, pressing down on him, twisting his thoughts.

And that's when he'd felt it—that strange, unsettling energy stirring deep within him, a latent force he'd always kept under control, hidden from the world. It was a power he rarely used, something he feared as much as he understood, something that lay beneath the surface, kept in check by years of restraint.

But that night, Harker's words had cut through his defenses, pushing him closer to the edge, drawing out the darkness he'd fought to keep buried.

"You have no idea who you're dealing with, do you, Detective?" Harker's voice had been mocking, filled with an almost gleeful malice. "You think you're so different, don't you? So in control. But you're just like me."

Kadin had felt his control slipping, the power inside him stirring, thrumming like an engine that had been left dormant for too long. The air around him had begun to vibrate, a low hum that seemed to resonate with the very fabric of the room.

Harker had laughed, his voice echoing off the walls. "Yes, that's it. I can feel it. You can't hide from it, Detective. It's who you are."

Kadin had taken a step back, his heart racing as he fought to keep his powers under control, to push the darkness back. But Harker's words had struck a nerve, cutting through his defenses, exposing the raw, untamed energy that lay beneath.

And then, something had snapped.

The room had erupted in a burst of raw power, the walls shaking as the very air seemed to come alive. Objects flew across the room, crashing into walls, shattering on impact. The floor trembled beneath him, cracks forming in the concrete, snaking out like veins.

Kadin could barely control himself, the power surging through him like a storm, overwhelming his senses, clouding his judgment. He could feel the energy pouring out of him, a force he'd never fully unleashed, a power that scared him as much as it thrilled him.

He remembered seeing Harker's face, his smug expression melting into one of shock, fear flickering in his eyes for the first time. The tables had turned, and for a brief, terrifying moment, Kadin had felt a surge of satisfaction, a thrill in seeing Harker's fear, in knowing that he held the power to end it all.

But that moment of satisfaction had quickly been replaced by horror as he realized what he'd done. The room was in shambles, the walls cracked, the air thick with dust and debris. Harker lay on the floor, barely conscious, his body battered and bruised.

Kadin had staggered back, the weight of what he'd unleashed crashing down on him. The power had faded, leaving him feeling drained, hollow, and filled with a deep, overwhelming shame.

He hadn't just used his power; he'd lost control, allowed the darkness within him to take over. And in that moment, he'd seen a glimpse of what he could become if he let go, if he allowed the power to consume him.

The Harker incident had been covered up, the details buried, the true extent of what had happened hidden from the official reports. Only Waller knew the full truth, the chief had helped him keep the incident quiet, understanding that Kadin was not just any detective, that his abilities came with risks few could understand.

But Kadin had never forgotten. The memory of that night had haunted him, a constant reminder of the darkness he carried, the power he kept locked away, hidden behind walls of restraint and control.

Kadin snapped back to the present, his body tensing as he felt the cold wind on his skin, the city's familiar sounds filling his ears. He stood still for a moment, his breath coming in short, shallow bursts as the memory faded, leaving him with a lingering sense of unease.

The Philly Ripper had sensed it, the same darkness he'd tried so hard to bury. She'd spoken as if she knew, as if she'd seen through his carefully constructed walls, exposed the truth he'd spent years hiding. And he couldn't shake the feeling that she was trying to push him, to force him into another Harker moment, to bring out the very thing he feared most.

He continued down the street, his steps slower, more measured, his mind racing. The Ripper's taunts, her threats, they were more than just a killer's sick game. She was targeting him, testing him, and he was beginning to wonder if this was about more than her crimes. If she saw him as a challenge, something to break, to corrupt.

The memory of Harker's face flashed in his mind, the look of fear in his eyes as Kadin had lost control. He clenched his fists, his jaw tight. He couldn't let that happen again. He couldn't let the Ripper pull him into the darkness, to push him to the point where he lost himself.

But as he walked through the city's streets, he felt a cold certainty settling over him. The Ripper was unlike anyone he'd faced before, and she was forcing him to confront the very thing he'd spent his life running from.

If he was going to catch her, he would have to face the darkness within himself. He would have to walk the line he'd been avoiding for so long, to confront the power he feared.

And deep down, he knew that this time, there was no turning back.

The day had dragged on, hours bleeding into one another as Kadin buried himself in his work. The Philly Ripper had gotten under his skin, creeping into his thoughts like an unwelcome guest, her voice lingering in his mind like a dark shadow. Every lead they'd followed had turned into a dead end, every new piece of evidence dissolving just as they thought they had something solid.

Kadin was back at his desk in the precinct, the noise around him fading into background static as he pored over the latest reports, hoping to find something—anything—that could break this case open. His phone sat beside him, silent for the moment, but his attention was drawn to it every few minutes, as if he were waiting for it to ring.

And then, it did.

A chill ran down his spine as he glanced at the screen. The number was unfamiliar, but he knew, somehow, who was on the other end. Taking a steadying breath, he picked up the phone and answered, his voice carefully controlled.

"Kadin Abell."

A beat of silence. Then, her voice drifted through the line, soft and unmistakably taunting. "Hello, Kadin."

He clenched his jaw, his fingers tightening around the phone. "What do you want?"

A soft laugh echoed in his ear, low and almost playful, but with a sharp edge that made his skin crawl. "You already know what I want, Kadin. But maybe we should talk about it in person."

"You've got my attention," he replied, keeping his tone steady, though his mind was racing. "Where?"

"The docks," she said, as if it were a casual invitation to coffee. "Pier 17. Midnight."

He glanced at the clock. That was less than two hours from now. "You expect me to just show up because you called?"

Her voice lowered, her tone laced with a deadly promise. "Yes, I do. And you'd better come alone, Kadin. If I so much as sense another officer near us, my next victim will suffer deeply. Much more than the others."

He could feel the weight of her words, the certainty behind them. She wasn't bluffing, and they both knew it. The Ripper had already proven she was capable of slipping past their defenses, of getting close enough to him to make her threats feel painfully real.

"You're willing to risk meeting me face-to-face?" he asked, trying to draw something, anything, out of her that might give him an edge. "Why?"

A pause, and then her voice softened, almost as if she were amused by his question. "Because I want to know you, Kadin. I want to understand what makes you so... fascinating."

The word made his skin prickle. He took a steadying breath, his mind racing as he weighed his options. She was daring him to meet her, to come alone and face her on her own terms. If he refused, she'd make good on her threat, and someone else would pay the price. But if he went alone, he was walking into her territory, playing her game.

"Fine," he said finally, his voice steady. "I'll be there. Alone."

"Good," she purred, satisfaction evident in her tone. "I'll be waiting, Kadin."

The line went dead, leaving him alone with the quiet hum of the office and the weight of the decision he'd just made. He set the phone down slowly, his gaze hardening as he turned his attention inward, preparing himself for the confrontation that lay ahead. He could feel the pull of the darkness within him, the same force he'd felt during the Harker incident, lurking just below the surface. But he couldn't let it consume him. Not tonight.

When midnight arrived, Kadin was ready.

He made his way to the docks, his footsteps echoing in the silence as he moved through the empty streets. The air was cold, a biting wind sweeping in off the water, carrying the scent of salt and decay. The docks were deserted, an eerie calm settling over the rows of shipping containers and abandoned warehouses. Shadows clung to every surface, thick and impenetrable, and the dim lights above barely cut through the darkness.

As he approached Pier 17, he felt his pulse quicken, his instincts sharpening. Every nerve in his body was on high alert, his senses tuned to the slightest movement, the faintest sound. He couldn't afford any mistakes.

There, standing alone in the middle of the pier, was the figure he'd been hunting for months. The Philly Ripper. She was just as he'd imagined—tall, lithe, her face obscured by the shadows cast by her cap. Her red jacket stood out like a warning, the green sneakers almost absurd against the grim backdrop of the docks.

"Hello, Kadin," she called, her voice carrying through the silence, familiar and chilling. "Right on time. I knew you'd come."

He stopped a few paces away, keeping his expression neutral, his hands at his sides but ready. "I'm here. So let's talk."

She tilted her head, watching him with an almost amused curiosity, as if he were an intriguing puzzle she was eager to solve. "You're so... serious," she murmured, taking a step closer, her movements smooth, almost graceful. "Always so controlled. But I know that's not who you really are."

"You don't know a damn thing about me," he replied, his voice hard. "You think you can scare me, manipulate me, but I'm here because I want to put an end to this. You're not in control here."

Her lips curled into a smile, but there was no warmth in it, only a cold, calculating interest. "Oh, but I am, Kadin. You're here because I wanted you to be here. You're playing my game, whether you like it or not."

He took a step closer, his gaze locked on hers, refusing to let her intimidate him. "Then why don't you end it? Turn yourself in. Or are you just afraid to lose?"

Her smile widened, her eyes glinting with something dark and unreadable. "Afraid? I don't think you understand, Kadin. This isn't about winning or losing. This is about you."

She lifted her hand, pointing a slender finger at him, her expression unreadable. "I've been watching you, Kadin. Watching you struggle, trying to hold it all together, pretending to be something you're not. You think you're different, don't you? Better than me. But deep down, we're the same."

He clenched his fists, his jaw tight. "I'm nothing like you."

"Oh, but you are," she replied, her tone soft and dangerous. "I see the darkness in you, Kadin. The part of you that you keep buried, that power you're so afraid of. You think you can control it, but I know better. I know what it feels like to let go, to embrace who you really are."

He took another step closer, his voice low and filled with anger. "Is that what this is? You're trying to push me, to make me like you?"

She laughed, a sound that echoed through the empty pier, filled with a chilling amusement. "Oh, Kadin, I don't need to make you like me. You already are."

Her words struck him like a blow, the certainty in her tone cutting through his defenses. He felt a flicker of doubt, a shadow of fear creeping into his mind. But he forced it back, steeling himself against her manipulations.

"I'm not going to let you win," he said, his voice steady. "This ends tonight."

She raised an eyebrow, a flicker of amusement crossing her face. "Does it? Do you really think you can catch me, Kadin? After all this time, all these games?"

He took another step closer, closing the distance between them, his gaze hard. "You think you're invincible. But you're just a coward, hiding behind threats and shadows. You're afraid to face the consequences of what you've done."

For the first time, her smile faltered, a shadow passing over her face. But it was gone as quickly as it had appeared, replaced by that same cold, mocking expression.

"I'm not hiding, Kadin. I'm right here. And if you want to stop me, you're going to have to embrace the darkness within you. Because that's the only way you'll ever be able to catch me."

He could feel his anger boiling, a dark, simmering rage that threatened to spill over, to consume him. She was pushing him, daring him to lose control, to let go of the restraint he'd spent his life building. And he could feel the power within him stirring, like a coiled serpent waiting to strike.

But he forced it back, taking a steadying breath, refusing to let her win. He wouldn't give her the satisfaction of seeing him break, of watching him become the very thing he'd spent his life fighting.

"This ends here," he said, his voice low and filled with determination. "You can't keep running, can't keep hiding. I'm going to bring you in, and you'll pay for every life you've taken."

She laughed again, a cold, mocking sound that sent a shiver down his spine. "You think this is over, Kadin? This is only the beginning. I'll be waiting, watching, and one day, you'll see the truth. You'll understand."

With that, she took a step back, melting into the shadows, her figure fading into the darkness like a wraith. He took a step forward, but she was gone, leaving only the faint echo of her laughter lingering in the air.

Kadin stood alone on the pier, the cold wind biting into his skin, his heart pounding as he stared into the empty shadows where she had stood. He could still feel her presence, a dark, unsettling energy that clung to him like a second skin, seeping into his mind, his thoughts.

He took a shaky breath, forcing himself to calm, to push her words from his mind. But the seed of doubt she'd planted lingered, a nagging question that he couldn't ignore.

Was she right? Was he like her, drawn to the darkness, to the power he'd kept hidden for so long?

As he turned to leave the pier, he knew one thing for certain—she wouldn't stop. The Ripper was playing a game, one that he was now fully entangled in. And he couldn't shake the feeling that, somehow, she'd already won, that she was pulling him deeper into a darkness he might not be able to escape.

But he wouldn't let her break him. He couldn't.

Not yet.

CHAPTER 5

Later that night...
Kadin stepped into his apartment, shutting the door quietly behind him. The weight of the night hung on his shoulders, every nerve still buzzing with the adrenaline and frustration of his confrontation with the Philly Ripper. The empty silence of his home should have been a relief, a respite from the darkness he'd been steeped in. But tonight, it felt more like a trap, the walls closing in around him, and he could feel that familiar tension building up inside.

He walked toward the kitchen, his mind racing as he tried to piece together what had happened at the docks, her words still echoing in his head like an unwanted mantra. Her taunts, her insinuations about his power—they'd struck deeper than he cared to admit. He took a deep breath, trying to steady himself, to push her voice from his mind. He'd done it a thousand times before, forced himself to lock away the memories of the Harker incident, the regrets, the doubts. But she'd cracked something open tonight, and the darkness he'd tried to keep buried was threatening to surge back to the surface.

And then, like a knife driving into his skull, the pain hit.

It started as a dull ache at the base of his skull, but within seconds it erupted, searing through his temples, bright and hot. His vision blurred, and he stumbled forward, gripping the edge of the kitchen counter as the pain pulsed through him, making it hard to breathe. He clenched his teeth, fighting against the wave of agony, his fingers digging into the countertop.

He'd felt this before—these migraines, these brutal, blinding headaches that felt like his head was splitting open from the inside. They only came when he'd let too much energy build up, when he'd held back for too long. His power didn't just lie dormant; it simmered beneath the surface, a constant reservoir of energy that demanded release. If he went too long without using it, without expelling the pent-up force in his body, it would start to turn on him, backfiring in ways he could barely handle.

Another pulse of pain hit, sharper this time, a burning sensation that radiated from his temples down to his spine. His hand fumbled across the countertop, his fingers brushing against a small, familiar orange bottle. He grabbed it, twisting off the cap with trembling fingers, and shook out a single yellow pill. He brought it to his lips, swallowing it dry, his throat raw from the tension.

For a few seconds, nothing happened. He could feel the energy roiling inside him, pulsing against the walls he'd built around it, threatening to break free. His vision blurred again, dark spots dancing before his eyes, and he leaned heavily against the counter, his breath coming in shallow, uneven gasps.

Then, slowly, the pain began to recede. The yellow pill worked its way through his system, dulling the edges of the migraine, calming the storm inside him. He took a deep breath, feeling the tension ease, the sharp stabbing pain fading into a dull ache. His muscles relaxed, and he could feel the energy settling back, contained once more, though it still hummed beneath the surface, ready to be unleashed.

He closed his eyes, letting himself sink into the quiet, savoring the relief. The pills didn't cure the problem—they were only a temporary fix, a way to manage the side effects of his powers when they became too much. But he'd come to rely on them, a crutch that allowed him to stay in control, to keep the energy at bay without giving in to the temptation of release.

He opened his eyes, staring at his reflection in the dark window above the sink. His face was pale, drawn, the strain etched into his features. He looked older, worn down, like someone who'd been fighting a battle they couldn't win. And maybe he was.

The Ripper's words came back to him, a whisper in the back of his mind, taunting, insidious. *I know what it feels like to let go, to embrace who you really are.*

He clenched his jaw, forcing the memory down, shoving it back into the recesses of his mind. She didn't know him. She didn't know anything about the control he'd spent his life building, the walls he'd constructed to keep himself in check. She wanted him to lose control, to unleash the power he held within him, but he wouldn't give her that satisfaction.

He turned away from the window, gripping the edge of the sink as he steadied himself. His body still thrummed with energy, a restless, potent force that pulsed beneath his skin, waiting, urging him to release it. He knew he couldn't keep holding it in forever; the energy would continue to build, pushing against his restraints until he had no choice but to let it out.

But that was a dangerous path, one he'd walked before and had barely survived.

Kadin's power wasn't just a gift; it was a curse, a relentless drive that demanded balance, a power that needed to be used, controlled, wielded with precision. He could absorb energy from almost any source—electricity, light, even kinetic force—and store it within himself, like a battery. But storing it was only half the equation. He had to release it, to use it in calculated doses, or the buildup would begin to take its toll, manifesting in migraines, muscle spasms, and, if left unchecked, full-body convulsions.

He'd learned this the hard way, back in the early days of his abilities, before he understood the limits of his own power. He remembered the first time he'd let the energy build too high, the way his body had rebelled, the pain and chaos that had erupted within him. It had been a lesson in humility, a brutal reminder that his powers weren't just something he could turn on and off at will. They were a part of him, a living, breathing force that required constant vigilance, discipline.

Kadin took another steadying breath, his fingers releasing their grip on the sink. The pill had dulled the worst of the pain, but he knew it was only a matter of time before it returned. He would need to find a way to release the energy, to use his powers in a controlled environment, something he could do without putting others at risk. But with the Ripper on the loose, taunting him, he hadn't had the luxury of focusing on his own needs.

The Ripper. Her face flashed in his mind, that mocking smile, the confidence in her voice as she'd taunted him at the docks. She'd spoken as if she understood him, as if she knew what it was like to carry this burden, this power. And maybe she did. Maybe she had abilities of her own, powers that mirrored his own, a dark reflection of the potential he kept locked away.

The thought sent a shiver through him. If she was like him, if she understood the lure of power, the temptation to let go, then he was dealing with a threat far more dangerous than he'd realized. She wasn't just a killer; she was someone who thrived on control, on pushing boundaries, on testing the limits of her own abilities. And she was watching him, studying him, as if she were waiting for him to slip, to fall into the darkness she'd embraced.

But he wouldn't let her win. He wouldn't let her drag him down, force him to become the very thing he feared. He had spent years building his control, learning to channel his powers in precise, calculated ways. And he would use that control to stop her, to end her reign of terror once and for all.

Kadin walked over to the small table by the window, his gaze drifting to the city lights outside. The buildings stretched up into the night, their windows darkened, the streets below bathed in the soft glow of streetlights. It was a city that held its secrets close, a place where darkness thrived, but he'd chosen to fight against it, to bring light to the shadows.

And the Ripper was the darkest shadow of all.

He picked up his phone, scrolling through his contacts until he found the chief's number. Waller had trusted him, covered for him after the Harker incident, and Kadin owed him honesty, even if he couldn't tell him everything. He dialed the number, waiting as the phone rang, his mind racing as he thought about what he would say.

After a few rings, Waller's gruff voice answered, sounding tired but alert. "Abell? It's late. Everything all right?"

Kadin hesitated, choosing his words carefully. "Chief, we need to talk. About the Ripper."

There was a pause on the other end of the line, and he could almost hear Waller's mind working, piecing together the implications of his call. "You've got something?"

"Not exactly," Kadin replied, his voice low. "But I think... I think she knows more about me than we realized. She's not just taunting us. She's targeting me specifically."

Waller's voice hardened. "What makes you say that?"

Kadin swallowed, his gaze fixed on the dark cityscape outside. "She wants me to lose control, to give in. I don't know why, but she's trying to push me, to get under my skin."

There was a heavy silence on the other end, and Kadin could feel the weight of Waller's concern, the unspoken questions lingering between them.

"Abell," Waller said finally, his tone softened, cautious. "I know you're strong, that you've got the control to keep it together. But if you're feeling like this is getting too personal, too close—"

"I'm fine, Chief," Kadin interrupted, forcing a note of confidence into his voice. "I can handle it. I just... thought you should know."

Another pause, then a sigh. "All right, Kadin. But keep me in the loop. Don't take any unnecessary risks."

Kadin nodded, though he knew Waller couldn't see him. "I will. Thanks, Chief."

He ended the call, setting the phone back down as he stared out at the city, his mind still racing, the tension still simmering beneath his skin. The Ripper had made this personal, drawn him into her twisted game, but he wouldn't let her win. He would use his power, his control, to bring her down, to end this nightmare once and for all.

As he stood there, feeling the energy pulsing within him, he made a silent promise. The next time he faced her, he would be ready. And this time, he wouldn't hold back.

The sharp ring of Kadin's phone jolted him out of a fitful sleep, dragging him from the clutches of a dark dream he couldn't quite remember. He reached for his phone on the nightstand, his heart pounding as he half-expected to see the unknown number flashing across the screen—the Ripper calling again, her voice taunting him, pulling him deeper into her twisted game.

But instead, the caller ID showed Chief Waller's number.

He exhaled, the tension easing slightly, though the urgency of the call still had him on edge. Waller wouldn't call this early without a reason.

Kadin answered, his voice low and rough with sleep. "Chief."

"Kadin." Waller's voice was grim, each word edged with a tension that made Kadin's pulse quicken. "We need you at the station. Now."

"What's going on?" Kadin asked, already swinging his legs out of bed, his feet hitting the cold floor as he straightened up.

Waller paused, and Kadin could almost hear the hesitation in his voice, the weight of what he was about to say. "We found out how the Ripper got that access card. And... it's gruesome."

A chill ran down Kadin's spine, but he forced himself to stay calm. "I'll be there in fifteen."

"Good. We'll be waiting," Waller said, before hanging up.

Kadin set his phone down, his mind racing as he quickly pulled on a pair of jeans and a dark shirt. He grabbed his jacket from the back of a chair, slipping his arms through the sleeves with practiced speed. There was no time to waste, no time to think about the implications of Waller's words. If they'd found out how the Ripper got that access card, it meant they were one step closer to understanding her methods—and, if they were lucky, stopping her.

As he laced up his boots, he couldn't shake the gnawing sense of dread that had settled in his gut. He'd seen his share of brutality, of twisted, dark minds who took pleasure in pain. But the Philly Ripper was different, and each encounter with her seemed to chip away at the barrier he'd built around himself, as if she knew exactly how to get under his skin, to push him closer to the edge.

He left his apartment, moving quickly down the hallway and out onto the empty street. The morning was cold and gray, a thin fog hanging in the air, muting the city's usual chaos. He slipped into his car and started the engine, the rumble filling the silence as he pulled out and headed toward the station.

The drive was short, but his mind was racing the entire time, turning over the possibilities, the implications of what the chief had said. If the Ripper had somehow gained access to an officer's card, then she was closer to them than they'd realized. And if it was as gruesome as Waller had suggested, then whatever they were about to uncover wasn't just another step in the investigation—it was a message.

When he arrived at the station, he parked quickly and made his way inside, his footsteps echoing down the tiled corridor. The atmosphere was tense, officers moving through the hallways with a quiet urgency, their faces grim. Whatever the Ripper had done, it had left a mark on the precinct.

He found Waller in his office, the chief standing by his desk, his expression hardened. A large file lay open on the desk, but Waller barely glanced at it as Kadin entered. Instead, he gestured for Kadin to follow him.

"They brought the evidence up to the forensics lab," Waller said, his tone clipped. "It's better if I show you."

Kadin nodded, his face set as he followed Waller through the precinct and up the narrow stairs to the forensics wing. The lab was dimly lit, the overhead lights casting a sterile glow over the stainless steel tables and equipment. A few technicians were already there, glancing up as Waller and Kadin entered, their expressions a mix of grim resignation and quiet horror.

Waller led him over to one of the tables, where a large evidence bag lay, sealed and labeled. Kadin's gaze shifted to the contents of the bag, his stomach twisting as he took in the gruesome sight.

Inside the bag was a severed hand, its skin pale and mottled, the fingers curled inward. The hand looked as if it had been hastily severed, the edges jagged and raw, blood staining the skin and pooling at the base. But what caught Kadin's eye was the keycard clutched tightly in the hand's grip, the plastic smeared with dried blood.

"This is how she got the access card," Waller said quietly, his voice barely above a whisper.

Kadin felt a surge of revulsion, but he kept his expression steady, forcing himself to look at the evidence without flinching. He'd seen death before, had dealt with countless crime scenes, but there was something about this—about the deliberate, methodical brutality of it—that left a chill in his bones.

"Whose hand is it?" Kadin asked, though he wasn't sure he wanted to know the answer.

Waller's face was hard, his jaw clenched. "We ran the fingerprints. It belongs to Officer Danvers."

Kadin's stomach dropped. Danvers was a patrol officer, someone he'd worked with a handful of times, a quiet, dependable man who'd been with the force for nearly a decade. He was known for his steady presence, his dedication to the job. And now... he was just another casualty, another pawn in the Ripper's twisted game.

"She... she cut off his hand just to get the access card?" Kadin said, struggling to keep the anger out of his voice.

Waller nodded, his expression dark. "That's what it looks like. She wanted access, and she wasn't willing to let anything stand in her way. Danvers never reported missing his keycard, which means she must have... taken him somewhere else, somewhere off the grid."

Kadin took a steadying breath, his gaze shifting back to the severed hand in the bag. The sight of it filled him with a cold rage, a burning desire to find the Ripper and put an end to her reign of terror. She hadn't just taken a life—she'd mutilated it, turned it into a twisted symbol, a message meant for him, for the entire precinct.

"This is personal," Kadin murmured, almost to himself. "She didn't just kill Danvers for convenience. She wanted us to find this, to see what she's capable of."

Waller nodded, his expression grim. "And she wanted you to see it too, Kadin. This is her way of pushing you, of testing your resolve."

Kadin felt his hands clench at his sides, his jaw tight. The Ripper had been taunting him, pushing him closer to the edge, daring him to lose control. And now she'd crossed a line, taken an officer, someone he'd known, and turned him into a prop in her sick game.

He took a deep breath, forcing himself to calm, to focus. The anger, the hatred—it was exactly what she wanted, what she was trying to draw out of him. But he wouldn't let her win. He couldn't.

"Have we found Danvers's body?" he asked, his voice steady, though his mind was racing.

Waller shook his head. "Not yet. We're combing through his usual routes, his known locations, but so far, no sign of him. It's like she... erased him."

Kadin nodded slowly, his mind working through the possibilities. The Ripper was a master of shadows, slipping in and out of places without leaving a trace, her movements calculated and deliberate. If she'd managed to take Danvers without anyone noticing, then she'd been planning this for a while, watching, waiting for the perfect opportunity.

He forced himself to look away from the severed hand, turning his attention back to Waller. "What about the other evidence? Do we have anything that might point us to where she's hiding?"

Waller sighed, his shoulders sagging slightly. "Nothing concrete. She's careful, leaves little to no trace. And now, with Danvers's keycard, she could have been anywhere in the station without us knowing."

The weight of Waller's words settled heavily on Kadin. The Ripper was slipping through their defenses, using their own tools against them, and now she'd crossed a line that few dared to cross. She'd made it personal, turned her vendetta into a twisted, bloody message that they couldn't ignore.

Kadin took a deep breath, his resolve hardening. "We need to find her, Chief. And we need to do it fast."

Waller nodded, his gaze steady. "I know, Abell. I know."

As they left the forensics lab, Kadin felt a renewed sense of determination settle over him. The Ripper had pushed him, taunted him, drawn him into her web, but she'd underestimated his resolve. He'd been through darkness before, had faced his own demons and come out the other side.

But this wasn't just about him anymore. This was about Danvers, about the other lives she'd taken, the families she'd torn apart. She was a predator, a force of chaos and destruction, and he couldn't let her continue.

They returned to Waller's office, and Kadin sank into a chair across from the chief's desk, his mind already racing with possibilities, plans, strategies. He knew he would need every ounce of his power, his control, if he was going to catch her. And he knew he couldn't afford any mistakes.

To be continued...

Milton Keynes UK
Ingram Content Group UK Ltd.
UKHW032058231124
451423UK00013B/949